A NORTH-SOUTH PAPERBACK

Critical praise for

Lila's Little Dinosaur

"Make room on the beginning-reader shelves for this delightful story. . . . De Wolf's watercolor cartoons clarify the action for young listeners and broaden the humor. . . . A gem . . . a guaranteed read-aloud hit."   *School Library Journal*

"This easy reader has all the qualities necessary for success: a clever little heroine, dinosaur lore, and an adorable rainbow-colored baby dinosaur that only children can see."   *Kirkus*

Wolfram Hänel
LILA'S LITTLE DINOSAUR

ILLUSTRATED BY
Alex de Wolf

Translated by J. Alison James

North-South Books

New York / London

Copyright © 1994 by Nord-Süd Verlag AG, Gossau Zürich, Switzerland
First published in Switzerland under the title *Lila und der regenbogenbunte Dinosaurier*
English translation copyright © 1994 by North-South Books Inc.

First published in the United States, Great Britain, Canada,
Australia, and New Zealand in 1994 by North-South Books,
an imprint of Nord-Süd Verlag AG, Gossau Zürich, Switzerland.
First paperback edition published in 1995.

Distributed in the United States by North-South Books Inc., New York.

Library of Congress Cataloging-in-Publication Data
Hänel, Wolfram.
[Lila und der regenbogenbunte Dinosaurier. English]
Lila's little dinosaur / Wolfram Hänel; illustrated by Alex de Wolf;
translated by J. Alison James.
Summary: When her father takes her to the museum,
Lila, who likes dinosaurs more than anything else, finds a little live
dinosaur who becomes so fond of her that he follows her home.
[1. Dinosuars—Fiction.] I. James, J. Alison.
II. Wolf, Alex de, ill. III. Title.
PZ7.H1928Li 1994
[E]—dc20 94-5065

ISBN 1-55858-310-6 (TRADE BINDING)
3 5 7 9 11 TB 10 8 6 4 2
ISBN 1-55858-311-4 (LIBRARY BINDING)
3 5 7 9 11 LB 10 8 6 4 2
ISBN 1-55858-522-2 (PAPERBACK)
1 3 5 7 9 PB 10 8 6 4 2

A CIP catalogue record for this book is available
from The British Library.
Printed in Belgium

It all started last Wednesday.

There was a notice in the paper:

DINOSAURS IN MOTION
at the Museum of Natural History

Now, Lila was exactly seven and a half years old, and she liked dinosaurs more than anything. More than cauliflower with melted cheese. More than running around barefoot in the rain. More than listening to loud music. More than frogs and hedgehogs and tigers and bears. Dinosaurs were the best.

So as soon as she saw the paper, Lila said, "I'm going!"

But Lila's mother had to go to work, and Lila's father did not feel like going to the museum on his day off.

"But I've *got* to go!" Lila said. She read the paper aloud: " 'A once-in-a-lifetime exhibit. See dinosaurs as they actually were!' " Lila showed the picture to her father. "I will never have another chance to see a dinosaur move. They're extinct, you know."

Somehow she convinced him.

"Okay, okay," he said.

So Lila's father picked her up from school.

On the way to the museum, Lila filled her father in on dinosaur facts. "They ate plants, mostly. Fern fronds, and sometimes even small trees. Some were meat eaters. But they didn't eat people."

"Of course, that's obvious," Lila went
on, "because people did not exist when
the dinosaurs were on the planet."

"I see what you mean," Lila's father
said. She could tell that he was getting
excited about the exhibit.

The museum was packed. Huge
dinosaurs loomed overhead, and
hundreds of children and parents
crowded in to see them. The dinosaurs
were not real, of course, but they looked
and sounded real. The exhibit was dark,
but lights flashed across the dinosaurs.
Then rumbling roars came from the
speakers. It was pretty scary, but Lila
thought it was terrific.

She poked her father in the side.
"See," she said. "That's a tyrannosaurus.
It's a meat eater. That big one over there
is an apatosaurus. It is a plant eater.

"And that is stegosaurus. See the plates? They collected heat from the sun," Lila said. "And over there is a styracosaurus. That means *spiked lizard*."

Lila's father looked around in confusion.

"Let's see if I've got these names," he said. "That big one is the pattysaurus. And the fierce looking one is a sty…ranno-saurus, and the one with the plates is a te…tego…?"

"Wrong!" laughed Lila. "Apatosaurus, tyrannosaurus, stegosaurus and styracosaurus. Got that?"

"I'll never get it!" cried Lila's father, tearing his hair.

Lila decided he looked a little like a dinosaur himself. Like a little dinosaur baby that had just hatched from its egg. When she told him, she shrieked with laughter. She couldn't stop laughing. But Lila's father did not think it was funny at all.

Suddenly the tyrannosaurus opened its gigantic mouth and roared. Its eyes blinked, and its head turned. Then, behind it, the styracosaurus rumbled to life. It cried a loud call and shook its thorny head. Stegosaurus swung its spiked tail, and apatosaurus swooped its long neck. Lila's father ducked his head.

"They don't eat people," Lila reminded him.

An old woman shook her umbrella at
the tyrannosaurus. "Stop that!" she cried.
"Stop that at once!"

It roared and blinked and turned its
head again.

"She's lucky that tyrannosaurus isn't
real," whispered Lila.

"I know," said Lila's father, taking a deep breath. "It is all an illusion. It is done with wires and electricity and cables. But it looks real, doesn't it?"

Lila got the feeling that her father was losing interest in the dinosaur museum. And she was right.

"It's time to go home now, Lila," he said, and he turned to go.

"Oh please, Daddy," she said. "Just another minute. I only want to find out how they work." And before he could answer...

Lila had crawled under the rope and disappeared behind the gigantic legs of the tyrannosaurus. At the base of the dinosaur's tail, there was an opening. Lila gazed in amazement at the wires and fuses and switches.

"So that's how it works," whispered Lila, and she listened to the hum and the clicks and the buzzes from the belly of the dinosaur. But there was another noise, a soft squeaking, that did not sound as if it was coming from one of the machines....

Suddenly Lila felt something wet and cold on her leg. Shocked, she sprang back and almost stepped on something, something that looked at her with a friendly expression, and wagged his tail. He was a tiny dinosaur.

A REAL dinosaur, not a battery-operated model! A real, tiny dinosaur, about the size of a small dog. The most amazing thing about him was that he glowed, in stripes, like a rainbow.

The little dinosaur kept wagging his tail, and tried to lick Lila's leg again.

"Hey," said Lila softly, "stop that."

The little dinosaur turned to go.

"I didn't mean go away," whispered
Lila. "Come here."

The dinosaur looked at her.

"Yes, come on. It's okay. Don't be
afraid."

The little dinosaur came up close,
sniffed Lila again, and then rolled over
on his back with all four legs in the air.
He wanted Lila to rub his belly!

"Boy oh boy," Lila said. Who would ever believe this? She was about to let the dinosaur suck her thumb when she heard her father call: "Lila! Where are you? Come back right now. I'm leaving!"

"What a shame," Lila said to the little dinosaur. "Look, I have to go now. But I'll come back tomorrow. I promise!"

Lila kissed the dinosaur good-bye on his cold, damp nose and ran off.

Lila did not look back, because she was sure that the little dinosaur would be sad, and she did not want to see him cry.

"So," said Lila's father. "Did you find out how they work?"

"What?" asked Lila.

"The dinosaurs," said her father. "You ran off to find out how they work."

"Oh, right," Lila said. "It's all just wires and switches."

"I knew it," said Lila's father.

Lila thought about her dinosaur.
She hoped he wouldn't be frightened all
alone among the noisy plastic monsters.
Tomorrow she would bring him
something to eat.

Then suddenly Lila heard a little boy call, "Look, Mama! Look at that dog. He looks like a rainbow!"

"What dog?" asked his mother. "Don't be silly. There's no dog."

"But he's right there! Look, Mama, he's right..." But his mother was already pulling him into the next room.

Lila turned to look. Across the museum lobby tottered the little rainbow-striped dinosaur. *Lila's dinosaur!* He smiled at Lila in a friendly way and wagged his tail.

"Where do you think you're going?" Lila whispered.

"Come along, Lila," said her father.

Lila turned around and whispered, "You have to stay here. What would I do with you?" But the little dinosaur followed her right down the stairs.

"What did you say?" asked her father.

"I'm talking to the dinosaur," Lila explained. "He keeps following us."

"Lila, your imagination is working overtime." Her father held up her coat. Lila decided not to say anything.

Lila and her father crossed the street. She looked back and saw the little dinosaur step into the road.

Of course, he did not look both ways before crossing.

Just then a huge van came roaring down the road. It was heading right for the little dinosaur.

"Stop! Look out!" shouted Lila, waving her arms. But the driver did not even slow down. The huge wheels thundered past the little dinosaur, missing him by a hair.

"That crazy driver, why didn't he brake!" cried Lila.

"Why should he have?" asked her father. "We were safely across the road."

Lila was confused. Could it be that she was the only one who could see the little dinosaur? But what about the little boy in the museum? Wait…maybe only *children* could see him.

Then Lila felt something wet and cold against her leg. Quickly she bent down and tucked the dinosaur inside her coat.

The tip of his tail stuck out, but Lila
thought that if her father couldn't see
the dinosaur at all, the tail didn't matter.
The little dinosaur curled up inside Lila's
coat and happily sucked on her thumb.

A minute later Lila's father wrinkled his nose and looked around. "What is that horrible smell?" he asked.

Then Lila noticed it too. The little dinosaur did smell pretty bad. Like old fish and rotten bananas!

"I don't know," said Lila. "I can't smell anything."

And then the dinosaur started to squirm around under Lila's coat. He growled loudly. He wanted to get out.

"What is that growling?" asked Lila's father.

"My tummy," said Lila quickly. "I'm hungry."

When they got home, Lila went
straight to the kitchen.

She got a carton of milk from the
refrigerator. But what would the little
dinosaur eat? Hot dogs? Spaghetti? Or
was he a plant eater? Would he eat the
fern in the bathroom?

"You know what?" said Lila. "Let's just have some of Grandmother's shortbread. That's always good."

So they sat at the table and ate shortbread and drank milk and swung their legs back and forth. Actually, only Lila swung her legs. The little dinosaur swung his tail.

They couldn't have been happier.

Suddenly the little dinosaur opened his mouth so wide his jawbones cracked, and...

"What is it?" asked Lila.

He gave a little burp, and then he curled up on the kitchen chair and fell fast asleep.

"*Yuck!*" said Lila. "I should have at least brushed your teeth."

Lila's mother came in.

"How was the museum?" she asked
cheerfully. Then she wrinkled up
her nose and said, "What's that terrible
smell?"

Then she started to sit down, right on
top of Lila's dinosaur!

"Wait! Don't sit there!" shrieked Lila, and she pulled the chair away just in time.

Lila's mother fell on the floor with a thump.

"What do you think you are doing!" she shouted. "What was that for?"

Lila's mother was angry, so she sent Lila to bed and said she would not even read her a bedtime story. Actually Lila was rather thankful, for she had a lot to do.

First she cleaned out her bottom drawer. Then she stuffed in an old blanket and a comfortable T-shirt, so her little dinosaur would not get cold. She opened the window a crack so that it would not smell so bad in the room.

But when Lila's father came in for a
good-night kiss, the first thing he said
was, "It stinks in here!"

"Tell me," said Lila cautiously. "What
would you think of our having a
dinosaur? Just a little one, the size of a
small dog, and pretty, say with bright
rainbow stripes?"

49

"You're nuts," said her father fondly. "What would we do with a dinosaur?"

"He could sleep in my bottom drawer," suggested Lila.

"That's silly," said her father. "Now go to sleep. Good night." He turned out the light and closed the door.

Lila had to giggle.

Quietly she called over to the bottom drawer: "Good night, little dinosaur. Sleep well, and sweet dreams."

The little dinosaur growled in his sleep.

When Lila woke up in the middle of the night, the entire room glowed with gentle lights, like a rainbow!

"It's beautiful!" whispered Lila, and she fell back to sleep.

Lila curled up under her covers
and dreamed about her dinosaur. She
dreamed about taking him to school with
her. And taking him to the seaside in
the summer. All the other children were
amazed.

When Lila woke up, her first thought was of the little dinosaur. She couldn't wait to take him to school.

"Good morning," Lila said.

But when she looked over at the bottom drawer, it was closed. Lila jumped out of bed. Her T-shirt was there, but no little dinosaur!

She searched under the desk, behind
the curtains, between her books: *nothing*.

Had it all been a dream?

She *knew* she had gone to the
museum. And she *thought* a dinosaur had
followed her home. But dinosaurs were
supposed to be extinct.

And she had never read anything about *rainbow-striped* dinosaurs. Her father always said she had an overactive imagination.

Lila slowly went downstairs.

"Good morning," said her father with a big smile on his face. "Your mother and I have decided that you are old enough to take care of a pet. The way you were talking last night about a baby dinosaur made us realize that you might like a dog or a cat."

"Hooray!" yelled Lila. But then she thought, *If only the little dinosaur were real!*

Lila's mother came in. "What happened to the fern in the bathroom?" she asked.

"Did you forget to water it again?" asked Lila's father.

"No, it's disappeared."

But they had no time to look for the
missing fern. Lila was already so late for
school that her father had to drive her.

As she got out of the car, Lila had
an idea.

"Listen, Daddy," she said. "Do you
think we could go back to the museum
this afternoon, just for a little while,
and…"

"NO!" shouted her father. "Not again!"

Then he sniffed, wrinkled up his nose,
and said, "Besides, after school you are
going straight in the bath." And he
drove off.

As Lila waved good-bye, she saw something that made her shout for joy! "There he is! He *is* real! Who needs a dog or cat? I've got my own little dinosaur!"

Wolfram Hänel lives in Hannover, Germany. He studied German and English literature and has worked as a photographer, a graphic artist, an advertising copywriter, and a playwright. Today, Wolfram Hänel writes plays and children's books, and often goes with his daughter to the Provincial Museum in Hannover. There they have a stuffed bear, a real bog mummy, and a dinosaur made of rubber that is fifteen feet tall!

His books for North-South include *The Old Man and the Bear*, *The Extraordinary Adventures of an Ordinary Hat*, and *Mia the Beach Cat*.

Alex de Wolf was born just outside Amsterdam, in Holland. He studied art in Amsterdam, and because he loved to draw children and animals, he would sit for hours  at the zoo drawing pictures. Alex de Wolf lives with his wife and their young son in Amsterdam. They have a garden in the country that is so overgrown with bamboo that it looks like a jungle. There they find frogs, rabbits, and hedgehogs, and who knows? Maybe someday they'll see a little dinosaur.

J. Alison James was born and raised in the United States, but has spent a great deal of time overseas. She studied English literature, German, and Swedish and went on to get a master's degree in children's literature. When she is not translating, she writes her own novels and children's books. Her translation of *The Rainbow Fish* won a Christopher Award in 1992. Alison James lives with her husband and daughter in Vermont, where dinosaurs lived many centuries ago. But something under the refrigerator smells like there might, just might, be a little dinosaur living in their house.